Babies

ROS ASQUITH

ILLUSTRATED BY SAM WILLIAMS

MACMILLAN CHILDREN'S BOOKS

There are **big** babies
and little **babies,**

do-lots and
do-little babies,

happy babies,
cross babies,

and "I'll show
you who's boss" babies.

There are **bouncy** babies,
funny babies,

and "oh, no,
not the honey!" babies,

wobbly babies, nibbly babies,

and **all** babies are
dribbly babies.

There are babies who
like teddies,

there are babies who
like muddles,

there are babies who
like bathtimes,

there are babies who
like cuddles.

Some babies
sneeze and chuckle,

some babies
squeal and wriggle,

but there's one thing that
all babies love.

If you tickle them, they giggle!

Let's try it: "Tickly wickly wee!"

There are many different babies,
but I'll tell you something true.

The baby that I love the best,
with all my heart, is . . .